WHEN It Starts to SNOW

by
Phillis Gershator

Illustrated by
Martin Matje

Henry Holt and Company

New York

Henry Holt and Company, LLC, *Publishers since 1866*, 115 West 18th Street, New York, New York 10011
Henry Holt is a registered trademark of Henry Holt and Company, LLC
Copyright © 1998 by Phillis Gershator. Illustrations copyright © 1998 by Martin Matje.
All rights reserved. Published in Canada by Fitzhenry & Whiteside Ltd.,
195 Allstate Parkway, Markham, Ontario L3R 4T8.

Library of Congress Cataloging-in-Publication Data
Gershator, Phillis/When it starts to snow/by Phillis Gershator: illustrated by Martin Matje.
Summary: Various animals tell what they do and where they go when it starts to snow.
[1. Snow—Fiction. 2. Animals—Fiction. 3. Stories in rhyme.] I. Matje, Martin, II. Title.
PZ8.3.G3285Wh 1998 [E]-dc21 97-40698

ISBN 0-8050-5404-9 / First Edition—1998
Typography by Martha Rago
The artist used gouache and colored pencils on cardboard to create the illustrations for this book.
Printed in the United States of America on acid-free paper. ∞
5 7 9 10 8 6

To Holly, Megan,
David, and Christy
—P.G.

For Théophile
—M.M.

What if it starts to snow?
What do you do?
Where do you go?

"I creep into the house,"
says the mouse.
Cold winds blow
when it starts to snow.

"I sit by the window,"
says the cat.
Big eyes glow
when it starts to snow.

"I keep watch,"
says the shiny black crow.

Caw

caw

caw

when it starts to snow.

"I look for seeds,"
says the sparrow.
Peck, peck, peck
when it starts to snow.

What if it starts to snow?
What do you do?
Where do you go?

"We fly south," say the geese,
"all in a row."

when it starts to snow.

"I build a lodge," says the beaver.
"The work is slow."
Chop, chop, chop
when it starts to snow.

"The water is chilly," says the fish.
"It's best to lie low."
Swish, shhh, shhh
when it starts to snow.

"I go in the barn," says the pig,
"if it's too cold to hoe."

oink
oink
oink

when it starts to snow.

"I wait for the farmer,"
says the cow.
"He's coming, I know."
Moo, moo, moo
when it starts to snow.

What if it starts to snow?
What do you do?
Where do you go?

"I hide my eggs," says the hen,
"so the chicks can grow."
Cluck, cluck, cluck
when it starts to snow.

"I fly high up," says the rooster.
"Listen to me crow."
Cock-a-doodle-doo
when it starts to snow.

"I stay here," says the worm.
"It's warm down below."
Wiggle, dig, dig
when it starts to snow.

What if it starts to snow?
What do you do?
Where do you go?

"I wear a new coat," says the stoat,
"a king from head to toe."
White winter fur
when it starts to snow.

"I follow the turtle," says the frog.
"Down into the mud I go."
Peep, peep, peep
when it starts to snow.

"I look for a place," says the deer,
"where the moss and grasses grow."
Leap, leap, run
when it starts to snow.

"I dive down the hill," says the otter.
"I go with the flow."
Slip, slip, slide
when it starts to snow.

"Look," says the black bear,
"The snow is deep.
Hurry, scurry!
Time to sleep."

Bat in a cave.
Snake in a rock pile.
Raccoon in a log.
Squirrel in a hollow.

Mole in a tunnel.
Rabbit in a hole.
Wolf in a den.
Chipmunk in a burrow.

Snow on the roof.
Snow on the ground.
Brand-new snow

coming down,

coming down.

I can't sleep
when the snow wants to play.

Three cheers for snow!